Promises for Kids
Verses to Learn from A to Z

compiled by Randy and Susan Jahns
illustrated by Debbie Bryer

Harold Shaw Publishers
Wheaton, Illinois

Unless otherwise noted as RSV or TLB, all Scripture is taken from the *Holy Bible, New International Version*. Copyright © 1973, 1978, 1984 International Bible Society. Used by permission of Zondervan Publishing House. All rights reserved.

Scripture noted as RSV is taken from the *Revised Standard Version of the Bible*, copyright 1946, 1952, 1971 by the Division of Christian Education of the National Council of the Churches of Christ in the U.S.A., and used by permission.

Scripture noted as TLB is taken from *The Living Bible* © 1971. Used by permission of Tyndale House Publishers, Inc., Wheaton, IL 60189. All rights reserved.

Copyright © 1994 by Randy and Susan Jahns

Cover and inside art © 1994 by Debbie Bryer

All rights reserved. No part of this book may be reproduced or transmitted in any form or by any means, electronic or mechanical, including photocopying, recording, or any information storage and retrieval system, without written permission from Harold Shaw Publishers, Box 567, Wheaton, Illinois 60189.

ISBN 0-87788-657-1

99

10 9 8 7 6 5 4

Printed in Colombia.
Impreso en Colombia.

The whole Bible was given to us by inspiration from God and is useful to teach us what is true and to make us realize what is wrong in our lives; it straightens us out and helps us do what is right. It is God's way of making us well prepared at every point, fully equipped to do good to everyone.

2 Timothy 3:16-17, TLB

A Special Note to Kids

Do you know that the Bible is God's Word? When you read the Bible, you can learn all the important things God wants to say to you.

This little book is full of verses from the Bible. It is not the whole Bible, but it has some important verses that have been picked out for kids like you. If you read these verses carefully—from A to Z—you will learn more about Jesus and his love for you.

But don't just read them once and forget them. Read them many times. Ask a grown-up to help you understand them. Look up the verses in your own Bible, and try to memorize them. Most of all, try to do some of the things that God asks you to do in his Word. It would be really great if you were able to memorize all of the big verses printed on each page. To help make it easier for you to remember, there is one big verse for each letter of the alphabet. You can say to yourself, "The letter *A*—Afraid. Psalm 56:3. When I am afraid, I will trust in you." Then the next time you feel afraid, you can remember what God's Word says about it.

God wants us to know his Word this way. The better we know it, the better we will know how to live each day. If you keep working on these verses, soon you will know the big verse for each letter of the alphabet. Turn to the back of this book and quiz yourself. There is a page with just the key word to remember for each letter of the alphabet.

The person who gave you this book hopes that you will grow to love God and obey his Word. There is nothing more important you can do with your life!

A Word to Parents

The purpose of this book is to provide a fun, easy-to-use method for learning some important principles from God's Word. For kids, the Bible may seem hard to understand or too big to tackle. This book carefully selects, from the Old and New Testaments, some key verses that speak to important spiritual concepts.

The book is organized under the outline of the alphabet. For each letter there is a key concept (for example: believe, grace, obey), followed by a few selected verses that relate to it. Many of the verses are well known and offer clear, understandable truths for children to understand and apply.

Encourage your child to read and memorize the verses using the themes and letters of the alphabet. By memorizing the theme with the verse, your child may be able to draw on a specific verse when faced with a life situation. For example, when your child feels afraid, he or she can remember the key word *afraid*, call to mind the verse "When I am afraid, I will trust in you," and begin to apply the truth to daily life. There is no better foundation to lay in your child's life than the Word of God. And there is no better time to learn that than when they are young—eager and able to memorize.

Older children will enjoy reading for themselves. Even children as young as three years old will be able to learn some of the verses with the consistent help of an adult. Encourage your child to remember the Bible references and learn to look up the verses in the Bible. As they grow and learn, they may want to add their own favorite verses to the section in the back of the book entitled "My Favorite Verses."

God promises his blessing to those who love and obey his Word. May this book help your child develop an early appreciation and understanding of the Bible, leading to a life of love for and devotion to God.

Afraid

Everyone feels afraid sometimes—even the bravest grown-ups. It is good to know that God is with us when we feel afraid.

When I am **afraid,** I will trust in you.   Psalm 56:3

The LORD is the stronghold of my life—of whom shall I be afraid?
Psalm 27:1

Believe

God's Word is full of great promises for those who believe in Jesus.

Believe in the Lord Jesus, and you will be saved. Acts 16:31

> All things are possible to him who believes. Mark 9:23, RSV

> For God so loved the world that he gave his one and only Son, that whoever believes in him shall not perish but have eternal life. John 3:16

Children

You are special to Jesus! Even though you are young, he cares about you and all other children.

> Jesus said, "Let the little **children** come to me, and do not hinder them, for the kingdom of heaven belongs to such as these."
> Matthew 19:14

> Even a child is known by his actions, by whether his conduct is pure and right.
> Proverbs 20:11

Day

We can praise God every day. He made each new day for us to enjoy and serve him.

> This is the **day** the LORD has made; let us rejoice and be glad in it. Psalm 118:24
>
> Day and night alike belong to you; you made the starlight and the sun. All nature is within your hands.
> Psalm 74:16-17, TLB
>
> Every day I will praise you.
> Psalm 145:2

Earth

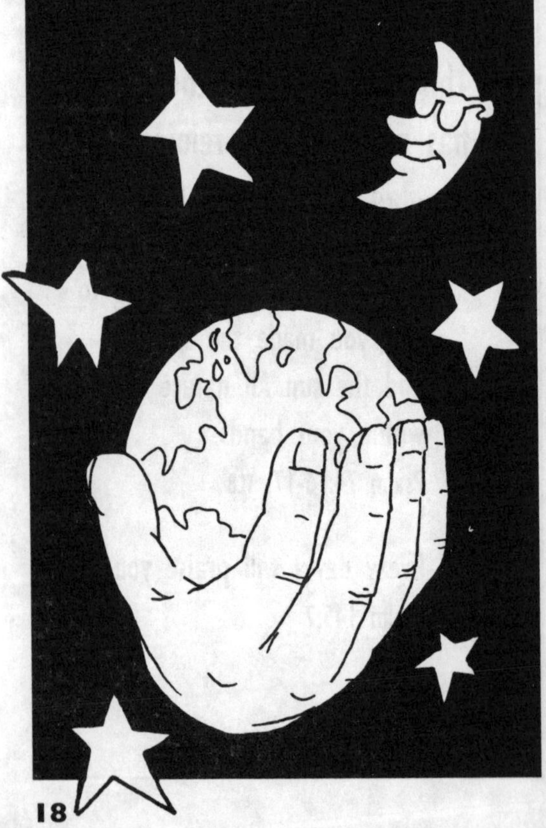

God created a beautiful place for us to live and take care of — the earth!

In the beginning God created the heavens and the **earth.** Genesis 1:1

The earth belongs to God! Everything in all the world is his! Psalm 24:1, TLB

How many are your works, O LORD! In wisdom you made them all; the earth is full of your creatures. Psalm 104:24

Forgive

Jesus offers to forgive us when we do wrong. And he helps us forgive others when they hurt us.

If we confess our sins, he is faithful and just and will **forgive** us our sins and purify us from all unrighteousness.
1 John 1:9

> Be gentle and ready to forgive; never hold grudges. Remember, the Lord forgave you, so you must forgive others. Colossians 3:13, TLB

Grace

We don't deserve all the good things God does for us. And we can't earn them either. But God gives them because of his grace.

> For it is by **grace** you have been saved, through faith—and this not from yourselves, it is the gift of God—not by works, so that no one can boast.
> Ephesians 2:8-9
>
>> From the fullness of his grace we have all received one blessing after another. John 1:16

Hope

I am special because God made me and because he is always with me.

I praise you because I am fearfully and wonderfully made.   Psalm 139:14

> I can do everything through him who gives me strength.
> Philippians 4:13

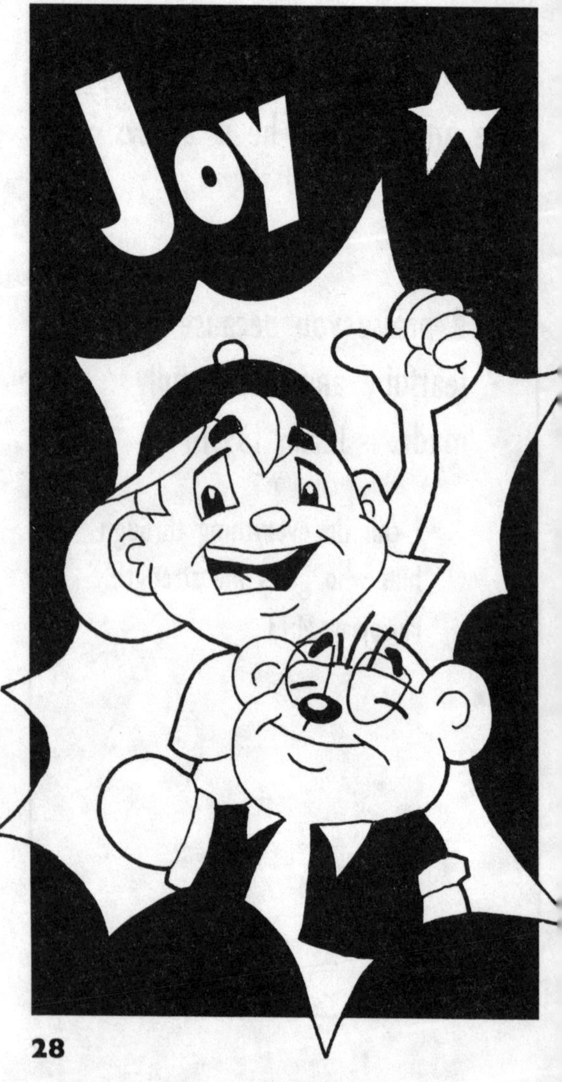
JOY

Joy is more than just being happy. Even when things don't seem to be going right, Jesus can give you joy inside. That's something to shout about!

> Be joyful always; give thanks in all circumstances, for this is God's will for you in Christ Jesus. 1 Thessalonians 5:16, 18

> Oh, come, let us sing to the Lord! Give a joyous shout in honor of the Rock of our salvation! Psalm 95:1, TLB

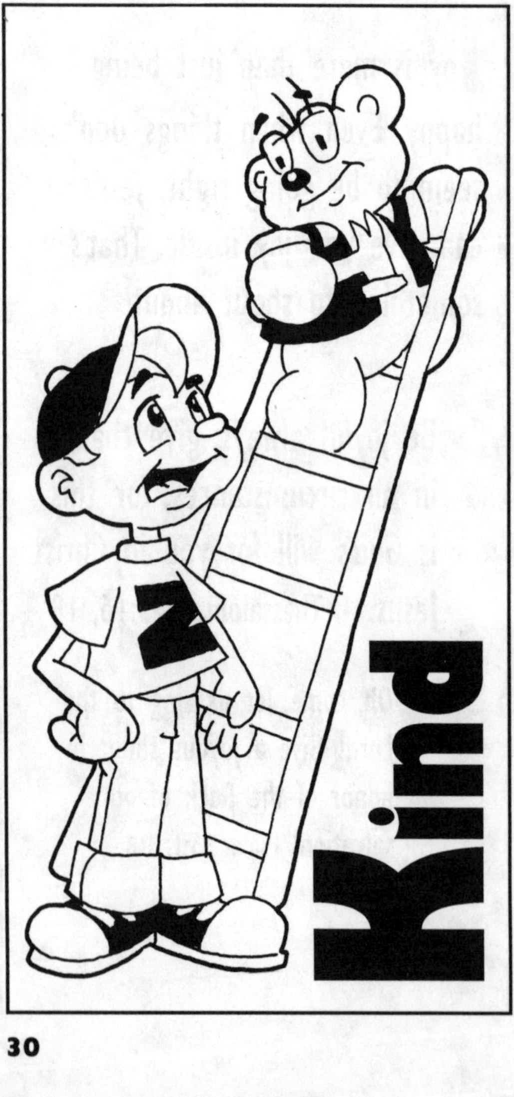
Kind

When you are kind to other people, you are obeying Jesus. He says that you should treat others the way you would like them to treat you.

Be **kind** and compassionate to one another, forgiving each other, just as in Christ God forgave you.
Ephesians 4:32

A kind man benefits himself, but a cruel man brings trouble on himself. Proverbs 11:17

Love

Loving God is the most important thing we can do in life. Because he loves us, we can love him and others, too.

Love the Lord your God with all your heart and with all your soul and with all your mind and with all your strength. . . . **Love** your neighbor as yourself.
Mark 12:30-31

We love, because he first loved us. 1 John 4:19, RSV

Mercy

God forgives and loves us even though we don't deserve it. That's called mercy.

He saved us, not because of righteous things we had done, but because of his **mercy.** Titus 3:5

Be merciful, just as your Father is merciful. Luke 6:36

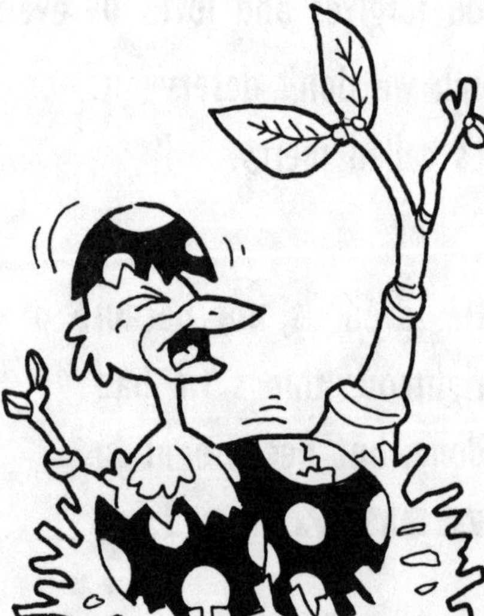

New

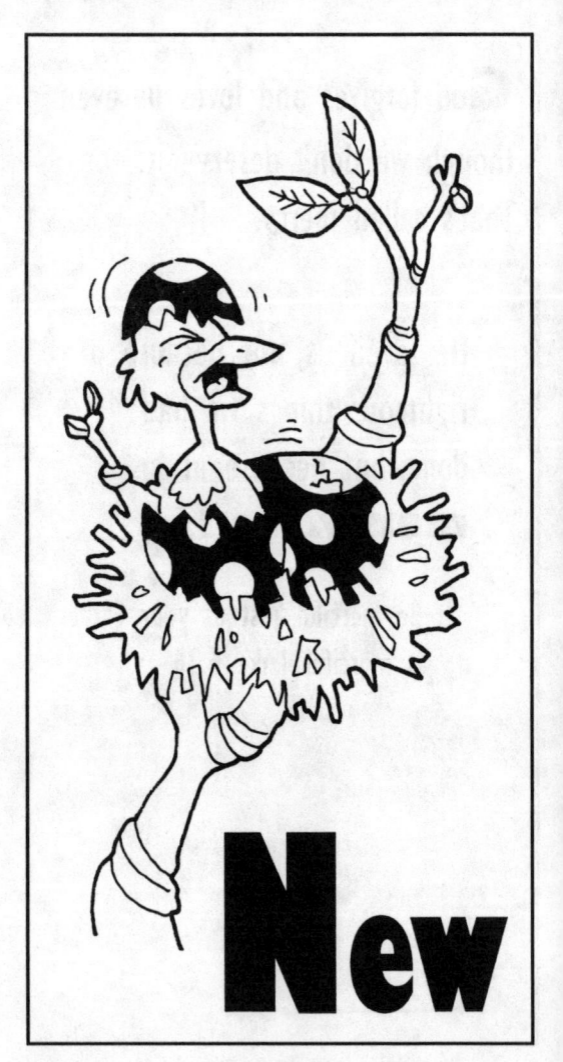

Isn't it exciting to have something shiny and new? When you become a Christian, Jesus makes you brand new on the inside.

> When someone becomes a Christian, he becomes a brand **new** person inside. He is not the same anymore. A **new** life has begun!
> 2 Corinthians 5:17, TLB

> Like newborn babies, crave pure spiritual milk, so that by it you may grow up in your salvation, now that you have tasted that the Lord is good.
> 1 Peter 2:2-3

Obey

It's not just kids who have to obey! Everyone must obey God and follow the rules. Obedience is hard sometimes, but the Bible says it's always the best way.

> Children, **obey** your parents in the Lord, for this is right. Ephesians 6:1
>
>> This is love for God: to obey his commands. 1 John 5:3
>
>> Obey the laws, then, for two reasons: first, to keep from being punished, and second, just because you know you should. Romans 13:5, TLB

Pray

Are there things you would like to talk to God about? God promises that anytime you talk to him, he will listen. That's what prayer is!

Always keep on praying.
1 Thessalonians 5:17, TLB

The LORD is far from the wicked but he hears the prayer of the righteous. Proverbs 15:29

If you believe, you will receive whatever you ask for in prayer. Matthew 21:22

Quarrels

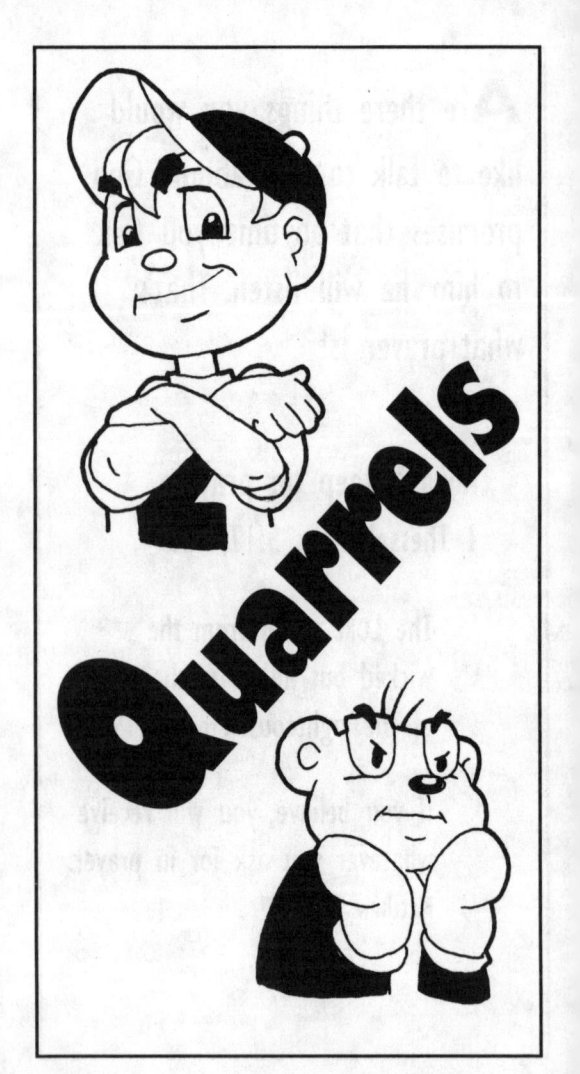

It's easy to get into arguments with people—but that always leads to trouble! A wise person stays away from fights.

> Don't have anything to do with foolish and stupid arguments, because you know they produce **quarrels.** And the Lord's servant must not quarrel; instead, he must be kind to everyone.
> 2 Timothy 2:23-24
>
>> Pride leads to arguments; be humble, take advice and become wise. Proverbs 13:10, TLB

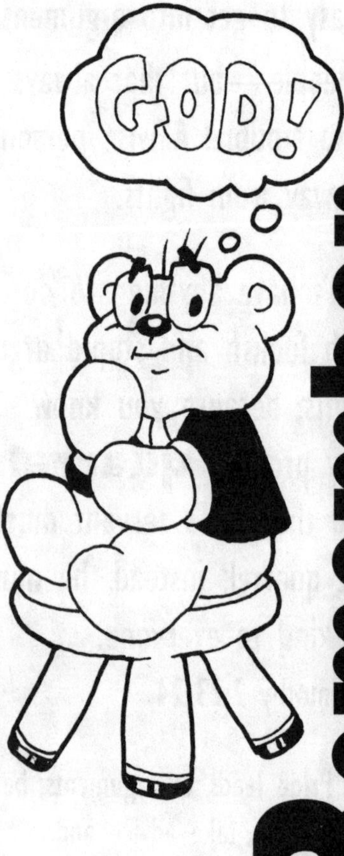

Rember

Get to know God when you are young. That way you will have your whole life to love him and think about all the great things he has done.

Remember your Creator in the days of your youth. Ecclesiastes 12:1

> Look to the LORD and his strength; seek his face always. Remember the wonders he has done, his miracles, and the judgments he pronounced.
> 1 Chronicles 16:11-12

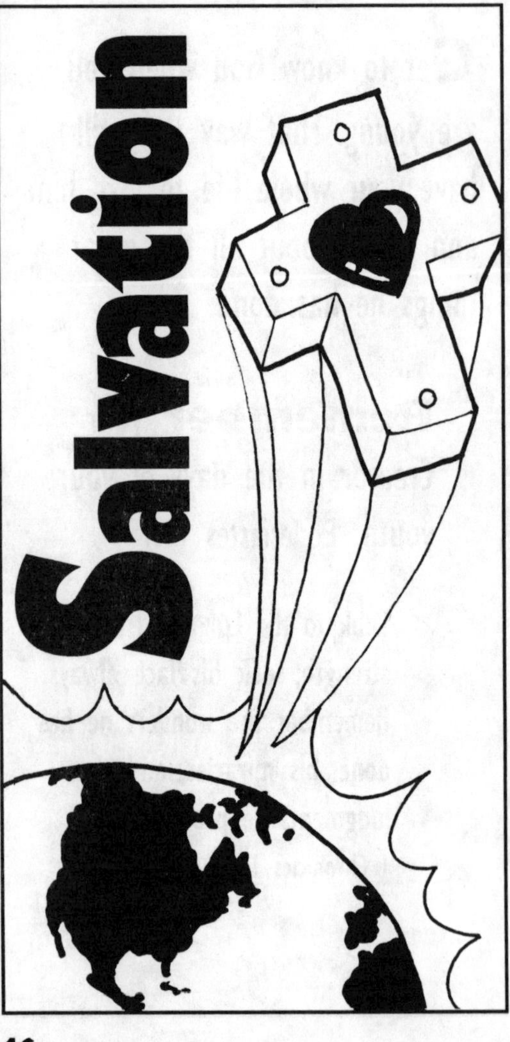

Salvation

Salvation means being saved by God. Only God can save us and give us new life.

> Let all the world look to me for **salvation!** For I am God; there is no other.
> Isaiah 45:22, TLB

>> I am not ashamed of the gospel, because it is the power of God for the salvation of everyone who believes.
>> Romans 1:16

>> For the Son of Man came to seek and to save what was lost. Luke 19:10

Trust

God always tells the truth. You can believe everything he says in his Word. If you trust in him, he will lead you and keep you safe.

Trust in the LORD with all your heart and lean not on your own understanding; in all your ways acknowledge him, and he will make your paths straight. Proverbs 3:5-6

Do not let your hearts be troubled. Trust in God; trust also in me. John 14:1

Understanding

Some people know lots of things, but they may not be wise. Ask God to help you understand the things that are important to him. That will make you wise!

> The fear of the LORD is the beginning of wisdom, and knowledge of the Holy One is **understanding.**
> Proverbs 9:10

>> We know also that the Son of God has come and has given us understanding, so that we may know him who is true.
>> 1 John 5:20

Voice

Even though you don't hear Jesus' voice with your ears, he still talks to you. When you read his Word, you will hear him speaking to your heart.

> Here I am! I stand at the door and knock. If anyone hears my **voice** and opens the door, I will come in and eat with him, and he with me.   Revelation 3:20

> My sheep recognize my voice, and I know them, and they follow me.   John 10:27, TLB

Word

The Bible is God's Word. In it God tells us how to love and obey him. Read your Bible—and do what it says!

I have hidden your **word** in my heart that I might not sin against you. Psalm 119:11

> Do not merely listen to the word, and so deceive yourselves. Do what it says.
> James 1:22
>
> Thy word is a lamp to my feet and a light to my path.
> Psalm 119:105, RSV

EXalt

God is greater than anyone or anything else. You can exalt God in your life by loving him more than anything else. He wants you to praise him this way.

> Let us praise the Lord together and **exalt** his name.   Psalm 34:3, TLB

> The LORD is exalted, for he dwells on high.   Isaiah 33:5

> But may all who seek you rejoice and be glad in you; may those who love your salvation always say, "Let God be exalted!"   Psalm 70:4

Young

Be happy that you are young! If you live the way God wants you to right now, you can be a good example to older people.

Don't let anyone look down on you because you are **young**, but set an example for the believers in speech, in life, in love, in faith and in purity.
1 Timothy 4:12

> How can a young man keep his way pure? By living according to your word.   Psalm 119:9

Z
The End

Most things have both a beginning and an end. The alphabet starts with *A* and ends with *Z*. But if you are a Christian, God has promised you life that will never end.

> The world and its desires pass away, but the man who does the will of God lives forever. 1 John 2:17

>> For the wages of sin is death, but the gift of God is eternal life in Christ Jesus our Lord. Romans 6:23

- ☐ **A** Afraid .... Psalm 56:3
- ☐ **B** Believe .... Acts 16:31
- ☐ **C** Children .... Matthew 19:14
- ☐ **D** Day .... Psalm 118:24
- ☐ **E** Earth .... Genesis 1:1
- ☐ **F** Forgive .... 1 John 1:9
- ☐ **G** Grace .... Ephesians 2:8-9
- ☐ **H** Hope .... Psalm 130:5
- ☐ **I** I .... Psalm 139:14
- ☐ **J** Joy ...... 1 Thessalonians 5:16, 18
- ☐ **K** Kind .... Ephesians 4:32
- ☐ **L** Love .... Mark 12:30-31
- ☐ **M** Mercy .... Titus 3:5
- ☐ **N** New .... 2 Corinthians 5:17
- ☐ **O** Obey .... Ephesians 6:1
- ☐ **P** Pray .... 1 Thessalonians 5:17
- ☐ **Q** Quarrels .... 2 Timothy 2:23-24
- ☐ **R** Remember .... Ecclesiastes 12:1

- ☐ **S** Salvation .... Isaiah 45:22
- ☐ **T** Trust .... Proverbs 3:5-6
- ☐ **U** Understanding ...... Proverbs 9:10
- ☐ **V** Voice .... Revelation 3:20
- ☐ **W** Word .... Psalm 119:11
- ☐ **X** EXalt .... Psalm 34:3
- ☐ **Y** Young .... 1 Timothy 4:12
- ☐ **Z** The End .... 1 John 2:17

My Favorite Verses